From Meltdown to Mistletoe
By: Jessica Terry

This is a work of fiction. Similarities to real people, places, or events are entirely coincidental.

FROM MELTDOWN TO MISTLETOE

First edition. February 19, 2024.

Written by Jessica Terry.

To my family, my readers, my supporters, I love you all.

Content warning: brief mention of attack/death (off page).

ONE

"JALIL DUNN?"

He turned, and I was slightly taken aback by the annoyed expression on his face. Despite that, I grinned and took a few steps towards him.

"I'm Kia," I verified with a gloved hand to my chest when he didn't speak for a moment. "Kia Love. We went to high school together." I giggled. "Though I was a lot skinnier back then so you probably don't remem-"

"I know who you are," he grunted, returning his attention to the key he was wiggling in his lock. Cursing under his breath, he muttered, "What's wrong with this damn door??"

"Oh, yeah, seems like all the doors in this building are a headache to get open." I took a few more steps towards him. "Here, let me help you. There's a little trick to it-"

"I've got it," he barked, shooting a look at me that stopped me in my tracks. "Um, thanks anyway."

"Okay." I ventured another smile, despite his glaringly bad mood. And the fact that he'd turned his attention back to the difficult door lock. "Well, happy Christmas Eve to you!"

All I got was another grunt. Figuring I'd leave him alone, I just turned and headed down the hall towards my own apartment, marveling that Jalil Dunn was apparently living in my building. I wondered how long he'd been there; I'd only recently moved in myself after having to unfortunately give up my house thanks to losing my job and running through my savings until I could find another, which hadn't been as easy as I expected after being let go from the company I'd worked twelve years for. When I was called into my boss's office that day almost a year and a half earlier, I was just *sure* I was going to be getting a holiday bonus. Instead, I got the proverbial pink slip because of 'downsizing'.

Unfortunately that just kicked off over a year of misfortune. Aside from losing my job and my house:

Got into a minor car accident and I was fine, but the dent still remains in my back side door.

Someone stole my puppy.

My cousins dropped my television when they were helping me move, and proceeded to avoid me when it came to replacing it.

I caught some weird virus that had me laid up for almost two months.

My favorite aunt died.

Ecetera.

I was living in a tiny apartment but I chose to count that as a blessing, even though it was a downgrade from the cute bungalow I'd lived in for the past eight years. But hey, it beat sleeping in my dented car.

Everyone went through rough patches so I was determined to keep the smile on my face. It could've been worse. And it felt like things were starting to turn around some. Aside from having a place to live, I'd finally found a job. Being a server in a diner wasn't ideal but it was employment, so I was grateful for it. And being there all day on Christmas wouldn't be that bad; at least I'd have the evening to myself.

And, I couldn't say I was in a relationship but I was dating. Gary and I had just gone on our fourth date and – this is such a girl thing to say, I acknowledge – I'd just shared my cherry pie with him for the first time.

All right, I can almost *hear* my cousin Marlow in my ear telling me how utterly corny that was and reminding me that I'm in my thirties.

Fine, sex. Gary and I had sex.

And it was...fine. I didn't have super-high expectations going in but considering how hot he was, I surely expected better than I got. It was just very *blah*. One position, little eye contact, and kissing only happened during foreplay. And whatever mints he popped didn't totally cover the smell of the garlic prawns he'd had during dinner earlier.

But, it was our first time. All first times weren't great. And apparently he agreed that it wasn't exactly stellar because he suggested we get some wine before diving in for round two. Liquor delivery wasn't available in my area and Gary was iffy on where the liquor store was, so I offered to go, figuring it would be quicker. I was sure our subsequent romps would be much better after a couple glasses of wine.

The bottles in the bag hanging from my wrist clinked slightly as I jimmied my key in the lock. Once I pushed open the door, I grinned in anticipation as I stomped the snow off my boots before stepping inside.

"Gary, I'm back!"

The television was still going but he wasn't in the living room where I'd left him. Figuring he was in the bathroom or something, I unbagged the wine on my small coffee table before removing my gloves and tan puffy jacket, then toeing off my boots. Pulling off my knitted cap and shaking out my faux locs, I strode over to the bathroom and knocked on the door.

"Gary? You okay?"

There was no sound of moving around, running water, nothing. I tentatively tried the doorknob and frowned cautiously when it opened right up, and confusion took over when I found the tiny bathroom empty. Whirling around, I lunged for the door practically directly across the short hallway, both hoping and not hoping that Gary was already on my bed, naked and ready to go. But realization hit when I found yet another empty room.

He left.

I released a flabbergasted breath as I dropped onto the queen-sized bed, bouncing slightly. Why would he just leave without a word like that? I'd had my phone on me the whole time and he hadn't let me know of any sudden emergencies or change in plans. And when I scurried around looking for an actual note, there was none.

"I cannot believe this," I muttered, my cheeks flushing in embarrassment. Had I been *that* bad in bed? Sure, I was a little nervous and it might have made me a tad inhibited, but I certainly didn't think it warranted him waiting until I left to sneak out.

What a way to cap off my Christmas Eve. Ghosted after mediocre sex.

(And I should note that my Christmas Eve started with ruining one of my favorite pairs of sneakers thanks to not looking where I was going. Seriously, who steps in wet cement??)

I heard my phone ring in my purse and I rushed over to grab it, keeping hope alive that it was Gary with some kind of explanation. But it was just my cousin, Marlow.

"Are you still with Gary?"

"Nope." I plopped onto my oatmeal-colored chenille couch, half my face buried in one of the pillows. "He left."

"Wow, y'all called it a night already? I know you have to get up early tomorrow, but-"

"I doubt consideration for my schedule was the reason behind him leaving while I went to the store without so much as a text."

"What??" Marlow shrieked, causing me to wince. "He seriously ghosted you?"

"Seems so."

"And you're *sure* he didn't leave a note or anything? Maybe he had a work emergency."

"He's a middle school teacher."

"Oh." Marlow sighed, apparently out of pacifying justifications. "That asshole."

"You said it, I didn't."

"Yes, I know you don't like to cuss. But I think this would be a damn good time to make an exception."

"For what?" I sighed, pushing myself up and slumping against the back of the couch, absently looking at *Almost Christmas* that was still playing on the TV screen. It had become one of my favorite Christmas movies and Gary and I were *supposed* to watch it together. (And it's not like I *never* cursed...I just had to be either really pissed off or really aroused. There'd been none of that earlier with Gary, I realized). "When I'm done flying off the handle, he'll still have left without a word and I'll still be here with three bottles of wine I shouldn't have spent money on."

"Kia, I'm so sorry, cuz. Have you called him?"

"No. I hate to assume but my gut tells me this was him just taking the cowardly way out instead of it being for any good reason. And if I'm honest, it's probably for the best, anyway. I wish he'd handled it differently but Gary apparently realized he and I weren't a match like I did but was trying not to admit."

"Whew, I'm glad you said it! I thought that the first time I met him but didn't want to seem negative. But now that he did this shit, fuck Gary. Fuck him, the stupid goalpost-sized gap in his teeth and those raggedy locs. He ain't all that. And you had to pay for the wine, too?? *Hell* no!"

My lips quirked, trying to hold in a laugh. I loved my cousin for trying to make me feel better by downing Gary, though even in my affronted state I could acknowledge that I actually thought the gap in his teeth was cute and how gorgeous his locs were. They were almost waist-length and might or might not have been the inspiration behind me getting my faux locs. Thankfully I never told him that.

And me paying for the wine? Yeah, I couldn't manage to pretty that up. He didn't even offer.

"Well, what's done is done," I sighed, choosing not to tell Marlow about the subpar sex Gary and I had before he dipped out. I was embarrassed enough. "With everything I've dealt with this past eighteen months, this is minor. Oh, you'll never guess who I saw. Jalil Dunn."

"Jalil Dunn? *Ooh*, you mean the one that played quarterback back in the day? I follow him on social media but he hardly ever posts anything; I heard he went to the military or something. Where'd you see him? Is he still fine as hell?"

"He seems to be my new neighbor, unless he has a key to someone's apartment down the hall from me. And I admit I didn't notice his fineness; he didn't seem to be in the best mood. He was pretty short with me, honestly."

"Jalil always was kind of a grump. He *kept* a mean-mug. Some girls actually had bets on who could get him to smile the most throughout the school year."

"Seriously?"

"Yeah, girl. He was mean as hell back then and I guess he still is. It's too bad 'cause, *umph*, between those eyebrows and that body and those lips, he was delicious."

"Maybe he just was just having a bad day. I can certainly relate."

"Yeah, but you don't ever bite anyone's head off because of it or take it out on anybody. You always manage to keep a smile on your face, and I damn sure admire you for that, cuz. You've been through the ringer lately and I hate it; you don't deserve that shit."

"Thank you for that, Marlow. It's not just me, though. *So* many people are going through it with the economy being the way it is and everything being so expensive and the wobbly job market. I thought for *sure* that with all my experience, I'd be able to find another job in my field, but...at least I have something that pays the bills. For the most part."

"See there? I'd probably be a depressed doughnut-eating mess if I were in your position, drowning my sorrows in booze. Speaking of which, you want me to come over? I can bring you some dinner and we can polish off the wine punk-ass Gary had you go get for nothing."

I chuckled. "Thanks but that's all right. I really do have to get up early so I'll just save it for another time; maybe ring in the new year with it, if they don't have me working. I'm just going to polish off my leftovers from earlier and call it a night."

"Okay, then. Let me know if you need anything or change your mind and want some company."

"I so appreciate you. You've been right here for me; helping me get into this apartment so fast, replacing the TV your brother broke, even paying off one of my bills. I love you so much. I'll be fine; tomorrow is another day. And it's Christmas."

"Yeah, and you'll be serving burgers and eggs all day instead of being with your family. But I already know what you're gonna say so I won't fuss about it. Your luck is gonna get better soon, Kia. It's *got* to."

"I'm sure it will." It was something I'd told myself so many times over the course of the previous eighteen months that it was practically automatic. I was pretty much sure I still believed it. "Good night, Marlow. Love you."

"Love you, too, cuz."

I ended the call and sighed, momentarily leaning my head back on the couch before making a move to get up. I paused, glancing at the phone in my hand as if expecting to see a sudden message from Gary explaining himself, but of course there was none. I decided to call, just so it couldn't be said I jumped to conclusions unfairly. There could've been a perfectly good reason he had to leave so suddenly.

But it turned out my earlier suspicions about him taking the cowardly way out were correct, because not only did he not answer, he blocked me.

That stung. I could see if Gary and I had argued or something before I left but we hadn't. He actually kissed me like he didn't want me to go and told me to hurry and get back. Said he appreciated me.

Right.

I could feel the tears but I blinked them back. The only thing crying would leave me with was puffy eyes the next morning; it wouldn't change a darn thing.

Forcing myself to shake it off, I got up and shuffled into the kitchen, my mouth all set for the rest of my steak, shrimp, and truffle potatoes from earlier. I'd reheat my food, restart my movie, and enjoy both curled up on the couch before turning in. My night didn't have to be a *total* bust.

But my evening took yet another kick to the teeth when I opened the refrigerator.

"Did he really take my freaking leftovers???"

TWO

I YAWNED AS I PULLED my faux locs into a ponytail early the next morning, Christmas music playing from my phone as I got ready for work. I'd managed to (pretty much) shake off the disappointment and frustration from the night before, with Gary sexing me, ghosting me, blocking me, *and* taking my food, and I was determined to enjoy my Christmas.

I wasn't exactly looking forward to spending twelve hours bussing food around a diner, but *somebody* had to work the Christmas day shift, and since I was the newbie (and no one else wanted to), it fell on me. The idea of missing my family's holiday celebration at my parents' could've bummed me out if I let it, but at least I'd still be able to go by there when I got off, even though most of the extended family would be gone by then. As long as there was some oyster dressing left.

Once I was ready to go, adorned with some glittery eyeshadow over my honey brown eyes for an extra pop of festiveness and plenty of moisturizer on my peanut brown skin to combat the cold outside, I grabbed my things and headed for the elevator, making sure my apartment door was securely locked first. It was going to be a snowy day in Brodence, our relatively small city in south Georgia, and I was good and bundled up, but I actually loved the snow and wasn't above playing in it at my grown age.

My eyebrows shot up in surprise when I saw Jalil standing in front of the elevator, his eyes on his phone.

"Hey, good morning," I greeted cheerfully with a bright smile as I approached. "Merry Christmas to ya!"

I heard the soft grunt before he even looked up, and his expression remained flat when he saw me. If I didn't know better, he even inched away slightly when I stood by him to wait for the elevator. "Yeah, Merry Christmas."

"Got any fun plans for the day?"

"Not really." He looked away.

I glanced at him with a slightly confused expression. How could he already be so grouchy at five-thirty in the morning?

And one discreet sweep of his frame confirmed that he was, in fact, as yummy as he'd been back in the day. Yummier, really.

"I guess you're an early bird like me, huh?" I pressed, strangely determined to break his shell. Jalil and I were never particularly close back in high school but we had a few classes together and spoke on occasion. We were acquaintances, if anything. But that didn't mean we couldn't be friends now, could it? Especially if we were neighbors. "I'm heading to work but I'm usually up early, regardless. Hey, if you don't have any other plans today, you should-"

"*Look*, we don't have to do this, all right?" he cut me off, his head whipping around to me. His scowl was so intense it made me step back some. "Just because we knew each other over twenty years ago doesn't mean we're cool now. I've got enough friends and I don't want to feel obligated to shoot the damn breeze with you every time we run into each other just because we live in the same building. So if you don't mind, when you see me around here, just nod and keep it moving."

The sting of his words prompted tears to burn my eyes, but I forced them to stay put. He wasn't about to have me crying because he was so set on returning my kindness with meanness.

"I'll respect that," I croaked, adjusting the Santa hat I had to wear for work. "In fact, I'll do you one better and just pretend I don't see you at all."

Turning on my heel, I headed for the stairs, not even wanting to share an elevator ride with Jalil the Grouch. I didn't understand why he had to say such things to me but I refused to give it any more energy.

I'd told myself that working on Christmas wouldn't be that bad since most people would likely be with their families or on vacation or doing things more fun than coming to a greasy diner, but I was way off. As soon as I got there, I was urged to toss my things in the back and 'get my butt in gear', since there was already a table full of truckers hungry and ready for their coffee and pancakes.

And it was like this *all day*. Table after table, with surprisingly large groups, came in with their barrages of questions about the menu and substitution requests and specific recommendations for their food that they were *not* shy about sending back if they weren't met exactly. Talk about nitpicky.

By noon, my feet and back were hurting and my decision to stay up watching my favorite movie twice was catching up to me, and I'd lost track of the number of times I yawned. But – bright side – I had access to all the free (somewhat bitter) coffee I wanted.

I tried not to think about how my family was probably filing into my parents' house by then, getting ready to watch basketball and devour the feast my mama and aunties cooked; stuffed turkey, roasted herb chicken, mac and cheese, sweet potato soufflé, greens, and of course, my favorite oyster dressing. That wasn't even the half of it, really. And don't get me started on the desserts; red velvet, sweet potato pie, apple cobbler, lemon pound cake, all from scratch. My mouth watered just thinking about it.

But I reminded myself I wasn't going totally without. I'd had a whole ten minutes to enjoy my patty melt.

I'd love to say the day got better as it progressed, but I don't like to lie. Someone's child tossed their milkshake onto the floor, and guess who had to clean it up before someone slipped on it? Heck, I kinda did, myself, and had a nice tweak in my ankle as a result. I usually got breaks but since we were so slammed and I was the only one working the floor (they didn't bother scheduling anyone else because they didn't anticipate being that busy), that wasn't the case today.

When another group came in and bunched themselves into the back booth, gabbing to each other the whole time, I seriously tried to recall what I could have possibly done to deserve such a crappy Christmas so far.

Why them? Why today? Have I not been punished enough??

"Can we get some help over here? We're thirsty!"

Telling myself to suck it up, I took a deep breath and hurried over to the group of women, limping slightly, a forced but pleasant smile on my face and my order pad on the ready.

"Hi, Merry Christmas, ladies! I'm Kia, and I'll be your server to-"

"Wait, don't I know you?" the lady sitting in the middle of the group asked, her pointed finger hovering and her eyes squinted in recollection. Her pressed black hair was shiny and fanned around her shoulders as if done on purpose, which I wouldn't have put past her. "You look familiar."

The other four ladies looked at me with renewed interest. Or by the way some of their expressions shifted, scrutiny.

Then as if on cue, they all shrieked at once.

"You're Kia Love!" one of them practically screamed, as if I hadn't already given them half of that information. "Wow, you sure have changed."

Imagine that. It's only been twenty years.

"Damn, you're a waitress? I thought you were some kind of executive. That's gotta be embarrassing."

No more embarrassing than that hairdo.

"I guess you're taking advantage of it 'cause you sure have filled out. You were a beanpole back in the day. And are those braces? Who wears braces as an adult?"

Lots of people. Einstein.

"Y'all, remember that time she lost her shoes at the prom?" Charity, who'd never been very nice to me even though I hadn't done a thing to her, reminded the group. Her skin was just as pretty and dark as I remembered and her makeup was flawless. All of them were dressed to party. I couldn't help but wonder why they'd chosen to come there on Christmas, of all places. "And she had to wear a pair from the lost and found?"

I pursed my lips at the reminder of that humiliating night. I'd slipped my heels off when I was in the bathroom because they hadn't quite been broken in yet and were hurting my feet. I was in a stall but someone had come in and apparently thought it would be funny to yank them from under the door, giggling loudly as they raced out of the bathroom. I had no proof but I was sure one of them did it.

It was pretty embarrassing having to walk around barefoot, crying angry tears that someone would do such a thing. One of the faculty dug a pair out of the lost and found so I'd have something on my feet, but the only thing that fit were some hideous brown loafers. Didn't exactly set off the silver dress I was wearing. I parked it at a table with my feet hidden underneath the tablecloth for the rest of the night, which my date didn't love. And of course, word had spread already and more than a few people couldn't resist getting in a few jokes at my expense.

"Yes, well..." I said now, forcing my smile to stay put. "What can I get you ladies to drink?"

"Aren't you divorced?" Retta, the one with the boobs all the boys used to salivate over. "I think I saw that on Facebook."

Clearing my throat, I told myself not to get irked. Annoying customers came with the job. "I am. But that was years ago. So, juice, coffee, tea-"

"Didn't you marry Ernest? He was cute but a little corny. What'd he do, dump you?"

My face went hot. Ernest was my high school sweetheart. We married young, realized we shouldn't have, and divorced. There were no hard feelings and we were cool to this day. I was actually his daughter's godmother. But they didn't need to know all that.

Sick of all the questions, I stepped closer and informed in a slightly-lowered voice and more bitingly than intended, "Ladies, we are very full and *very* busy. If you still need a minute to decide, I'm more than happy to come back. But if we could save the trips down memory lane for another time, I'd appreciate it."

They all looked startled as if they couldn't believe my nerve. Finally mumbling their drink orders, they almost seemed dazed as I scribbled down the information and turned to walk off. I wasn't trying to be rude but I also wasn't trying to stand there forever on a throbbing ankle while they scraped up every unpleasant memory they could about me.

Just a couple more hours to go, I reminded myself as I got their drinks. *Maybe they'll chill out now that they see I'm not the same meek Kia I was back in the day. Just kill 'em with kindness...it's the only way I can get away with it.*

No such luck, unfortunately. Those ladies proceeded to run me ragged, just because they felt like they could.

The coffee was too hot.

They seemed to take turns finding "unacceptable" water spots on their silverware.

They needed more sugar than was in the container stuffed with it already at the table.

Not enough cheese in the eggs. Nor were they scrambled correctly.

There was something in their water glass (there wasn't).

The edges of their pancakes weren't crispy enough.

The cooks were past tired of their difficulty, and since I was the one that had to keep coming back there requesting something be changed or redone or substituted, I got the pleasure of their rebuke. Between them, my tormenting former classmates, and the other tables that needed seemingly endless attention, with no time to breathe between any of this, I felt like I was about to explode.

And when I got one ridiculous request too many, I kinda did.

"Oh Kiaaaaa!" Charity sang, loudly, as I was grabbing them the napkins they asked for (or demanded). "We have a problem over here, sweetie. Remember when I described the *exact* amount of pink I wanted in my steak? I said more 'blush' and less 'mauve.' This is wrong, *again*." She held up her plate, not even bothering to look at me as she and her friends held in taunting giggles at the obvious fun they were having. "I need it redone. And I want a *fresh* piece of steak, not them just throwing this one back on the flattop. Believe me, I'll know the difference. And I'd hate to have to dock your tip 'cause y'all can't follow simple directions."

I think I literally felt something snap inside me. That was *it*.

"You know *what*?" I snapped, throwing their napkins onto the table, making them all jump. "You want that steak fixed? I'll fix that steak!"

I grabbed a squeeze bottle of ketchup in one hand and a bottle of mayonnaise in the other and squirted both right on top of the steak she was still holding in the air, ignoring their mortified gasps, then snatched a couple of their spoons and vigorously mixed the condiments together, some of it dripping onto the table.

"That the right shade of pink?" I demanded, looking right at Charity as I dropped the spoons onto the nearest laps, making them shriek about their outfits being sullied. "I can add more mayo if it's not *blush* enough for you!"

Charity was just looking at me in utter shock as I moved on to Retta, who'd complained about her eggs more than once.

"These eggs aren't scrambled enough, right?" I yanked the fork from her hand and wildly chopped it through her eggs, sending bits flying and causing her to lean as far back in her seat as she could, her hands shielding her face, as if the egg bits were acid. "Voila`!"

They were looking at me like I'd lost my mind, and there might've even been a bit of fear in their heavy-lashed eyes that I couldn't help but enjoy right then.

"Too much ice in your water, huh?" I dug some cubes out with my fingers and dumped it into the apparently too-hot coffee from before, splashing it. "Two birds with one stone. Not enough salt on those fries? Welp, not a problem now!" I dumped practically the entire shaker onto the plate of steak-cut fries. "Oh, and you said this knife wasn't sharp enough, didn't you? I'll *gladly* rectify that."

"NO!" they all screamed, either holding up their hands or moving their knives out of my reach. They bunched up together towards the middle of the booth, away from me.

"I'm *done*!" I spat, breathing fire as I shot daggers at all of them. "I have tried to be nice and professional, but you all have seemed to make it your mission to give me a hard time and I'm *over* it! It is *not* okay to treat people this way! If you want to act like the catty *bitches* you were in high school, fine, but I'm not going to be your whipping girl while you do it! *I do not deserve this shit!!*"

It was then that I remembered that we weren't alone and everyone was looking at me with their jaws on their plates, and of course, a couple of phones were aimed in my direction, recording my meltdown. And because this afternoon hadn't sucked enough, who else was standing near the empty hostess station but Jalil, looking like he'd seen a ghost. At least he wasn't frowning, for once.

My chest still heaving, I turned and hurried towards the back before the realization of what I'd just done started to creep in, as I was sure it would eventually. Vinny, my boss, called out to me as

I stormed by him. He was looking as dumbfounded as everyone else at my behavior.

"Kia, what the hell?? Are you -"

"You don't even have to bother, Vinny; I'm sure I'm fired," I cut him off, yanking on my coat and grabbing my purse. I didn't need to hear him get around to saying the words. "I know you always say we should have thick skin out there but we also shouldn't have to be treated like scurrying monkeys for people's entertainment."

He just stood there looking at me, his expression unreadable. And I didn't need to stick around for him to make it plain.

"I'm sorry to leave you hanging like this," I muttered as I prepared to leave. "Merry Christm-ugh, what's the damn point."

I tried to go out the back door but, in keeping with the stellar day I was having, it was jammed and not budging no matter how much I pushed and kicked at it (and since I momentarily forgot about my hurt ankle, that was just another gold star on the day). So I had to go out the front, which meant facing everyone again, but I was still too keyed up to be embarrassed. I stomped right past Charity and her hens, actually proud when their still-appalled babbling ceased immediately and they leaned away from me as if expecting one last parting tirade. Good.

I groaned when I saw Jalil still standing near the exit. But, being a woman of my word, I pretended like I didn't.

"Kia," he called out as I brushed past and out the door. The cold wind hit my face like a hard slap as I headed to the car, my ankle throbbing as I tried my best not to slip on the occasional patches of ice littering the parking lot.

"Kia, hold up a second."

Ignoring him, I unlocked my car and yanked the door open, tossing my purse into the passenger's seat. I was inside and about to close the door when Jalil caught it, stopping me.

"Hey, you all right?" he asked, peering down at me. "I never thought you of all people would go off like that. And were you limping just now?"

"Why do you care?" I snapped. "I thought we weren't supposed to be talking. We're not cool, remember?" I tugged on the door with both hands, huffing impatiently when he kept his firm grip on it. "Let go of my door, please."

"Look...I'm sorry about this morning." Jalil actually looked remorseful, but I was unmoved. I was so over this day and just wanted to get from around people, especially him. "That was...look, let me get you home. I don't think you should be driving when you're this upset, especially in these conditions."

"No thank you. Wouldn't want you to feel *obligated*." I gave the door another yank, and he finally released it, swiftly moving his hand before I slammed it in the door like I tried to. Without giving him another look, I started the car and pulled out of the parking lot, leaving him standing there watching me.

I thought about going to my parents' house but I just went home, opting to call them later. I wanted to be alone when the realization that the little progress I was making was wiped out thanks to surely being unemployed again hit.

Merry freaking Christmas to me.

I didn't even try to stop the tears streaming down my cheeks as I limped to my apartment door. I was tired on every level. Tired of nothing seeming to go my way recently. Tired of trying to find the bright side and put a positive spin on everything, even when parts of me wanted to break down and have a full-on tantrum. Tired of forcing self-pep talks that were getting increasingly harder to believe. My energy was officially *gone*.

Christmas was usually one of my favorite days of the year but I just couldn't wait for this one to be over.

After a shower and putting on my thick around-the-house sweats, I felt marginally better. I got some ice for my ankle and parked it on the couch, planning to get my full money's worth on the wine I'd bought the night before. My stomach was rumbling for food but if I couldn't have my mama's oyster dressing and everything else my family had enjoyed without me, I'd just stay hungry.

But a timely call from Marlow fixed that. Once she heard about my abysmal day and that I was sulking and starving, she rushed right over with several foil-wrapped plates stuffed with food from the family dinner. I never loved her more. Unfortunately she had plans and couldn't stay, but she made time to get in a good tirade about Jalil as well as our taunting former classmates. That made me laugh some, at least.

I was enjoying my food when there was a knock on the door. Marlow and occasionally my parents were usually my only visitors, and they always called first, so I had a feeling as to who it was. The still-simmering petty part of me wanted to just leave him out there, but eventually I sighed and got up, hobbling over to the door.

Jalil stood there, looking contrite and – dang it – sexier than I wanted to admit. If I was all the way honest, seeing him there in his dark boots and jeans, black sweater, and gray coat with a scarf around the collar was waking up certain parts that were still mad from the previous night's subpar sexual experience with Gary.

But him being achingly hot didn't excuse him being a jerk.

"Why are you here?" I demanded, folding my arms under my breasts.

"I wanted to check on you." He looked me up and down and I hated how my kitty reacted to that. "Make sure you made it home safely."

"Well, as you can see, I did. Safe and sound. Now, goodnight."

"Kia, hold up!" He stopped the door before I could close it in his face. "I also wanted to apologize to you, again, for this morning. You didn't deserve that shit I said; I've just had a rough few weeks and I took it out on you. I'm sincerely sorry for that."

Some of my fire cooled. If anyone could understand that, I could.

"All right," I finally sighed, lifting a brief hand of concession. "I get it. Apology accepted, thanks. Have a good evening."

"Kia," he stopped the door again, actually looking nervous.

"Yes?"

"Can I make this up to you?"

THREE

MY IMAGINATION AUTOMATICALLY went ten different ways at that question.

"How would you do that?" I croaked, my throat suddenly dry.

"I can take you out," Jalil offered, taking a small step closer. "You shouldn't have to have your Christmas end up like this."

"That's...that's sweet, Jalil, but it's been a long day and I'm really not in the mood to get dressed and go anywhere. I've been on my feet all day, my ankle hurts-"

I yelped in surprise when he scooped me up and carried me over the couch, gently setting me down and giving me an up close view of those smoldering eyes of his.

"You shouldn't be standing on it, then."

Every part of me was screaming. His face was near mine. His voice was low and enticing to my ears. The all-too-brief feel of his strong body as he carried me was like a tease. I could actually *feel* his heat as he remained hovered over me.

His eyes locked on mine for a few moments before I whispered, "Um, you left the door open."

He glanced over his shoulder at it before returning his eyes to me. "When I close it, can I stay on this side of it with you? Or would you rather I leave?"

Leave? That's crazy talk.

"Jalil..." I sat up a little straighter and silently told myself to get it together. "Please don't feel like you owe me anything else. You apologized, I accepted. We're fine. And I'm used to entertaining myself."

"Same, but why do that when we can entertain each other? Unless you just sincerely want to be by yourself, I hate the thought of you closing out this Christmas alone, especially considering how excited you seemed for it this morning. I just want to hang out with you, Kia, that's all. I'm really not the asshole you probably think I am."

The way he had my body buzzing, that was *not* the descriptor I'd use for him right then.

"All right, then," I conceded, tired of trying to act like I didn't want the man to stay. "You can hang out for while, if you want."

I saw hints of a smile as he went to close the door. When he returned to the couch, removing his coat and gloves before he sat, I inched over to make room for him, my nervousness and arousal battling for position. I was alone with Jalil Dunn. The Jalil Dunn I might have drooled over a time or two back in the day, even though I was fine with it being nothing but a fantasy. I was no ugly duckling and I had boyfriends, but I wasn't very popular. As a transfer student, I didn't easily integrate into any of the already-established cliques. I just kinda did my own thing. And since I was 'the nice one' who didn't love conflict or drama, I tended to fade into the background.

"Did you get to eat earlier?" I asked him, motioning towards my half-eaten plate on the coffee table. "Not sure if you hung around to have something at the diner earlier but you're welcome to some of these leftovers. It's from my family's dinner. There's more in the kitchen."

"Oh no, I'm good, thanks," Jalil quickly insisted. "I ate with my brothers. I was actually at the diner picking up dinner for my veterans group."

"Your veterans group?"

"Yeah, I do volunteer work with the VA and there's a group of vets I spend time with and try to help out however I can. Most of them have been having a hard time since they got out of the service; trouble finding jobs, dealing with PTSD or other injuries, fighting for their disability benefits, all that. A couple of them don't have much family. And for some of the others, the holidays aren't the festive time it is for a lot of other people and depression hits them especially hard this time of year."

"Oh my goodness..." My hand flew to my chest, my heart aching at that. I hated to hear about anyone going through a rough time, especially during the holidays, but it was extra sad when it was our veterans. They shouldn't have had to struggle so much after serving our country. "That's horrible. Are any of them people you served with?"

"A couple of them." He looked ahead of him as he slowly rubbed his hands together, a thoughtful expression clouding his face. "It's, ah...it can be kinda hard seeing them going through it. Especially when I'm..."

I straightened, getting it. "When you're not."

"Yeah." He heaved a sigh, his eyes dropping to his hands. "I've had it pretty good since I got out. I try to help out as much as I can but it never feels like enough, you know? It just *pisses* me off when I see people who volunteered to put their life on the line for this fucked up country having to live in a shelter or be given the runaround for benefits every human should get regardless. And I admit I don't always do the best job of leaving my frustration at the door when I leave them."

His grouchiness made so much more sense now. Yeah, how he treated me earlier was still jacked up, but I could certainly empathize the reasoning behind it. If anything, the fact that he felt so deeply for his fellow veterans was endearing.

"I get it," I ventured, inching a teeny bit closer to him. My hand went to his back without thinking, giving it a few comforting sweeps. "And I'm so sorry *any* of you are going through tough times after what you've already been through. But you shouldn't feel guilty that you're not struggling, Jalil. Life might not have dealt you the same unfortunate hand that has them, but you're sharing your proverbial winnings with them. Your time, your compassion, your energy and efforts towards making their lives better. All of that is invaluable and I'm sure they recognize that."

I could see the glint of disbelief when he looked over at me. "You really believe that?"

"Of course. Look, life can suck sometimes; I'm as aware of that as anyone. I've lost so much this past year and a half but – and I know this is easier said than done – you just have to shift your perspective. It's almost a daily thing for me. Things might not be ideal but...sometimes we get *so* hung up on all the bad things happening that we gloss over the good things. There's *always* something to be thankful for, I believe."

"Wow." He turned his upper body towards me, actually looking amazed. "I've heard people spout this kind of stuff before but I admit I usually think it's bullshit. But you seem genuine with it; like you have this aura around you that's almost...and I can't believe I'm about to say this...*angelic*."

I blushed, flattered but humbled at the compliment. "That's sweet but believe me, I'm no angel."

"You seem closer to one than anybody I've been around in a long while. This is a far cry from the woman I saw flipping out and tossing food around at the diner earlier."

My cheeks flushed harder at the reminder and my hand fell back to my lap. "Not my proudest moment, I admit. I always try to turn the other cheek, but...a person can only take so much."

"Seeing who you were dealing with, I can understand why you went off. Charity and her little posse have always been a pain in the ass. It's too bad they apparently haven't matured much since high school."

"True. Still, though, I almost *never* lose it like that." My nails scraped my palm. "But if I'm honest, it felt pretty good to finally put them in their place, even if it did likely cost me my job. I can only imagine what they said about me after I left."

"Who cares what they said. I'm just glad you're good after all that and not in here kicking yourself over it."

"Surprisingly, I'm not. I might be a nice person but I'm nobody's doormat. And I'm as good as can be expected; better than I was when I left there, at least. It's, um, it's nice of you to care about it."

"I'm not a monster, Kia." He gazed at me a moment before his eyes dropped. "Even though I acted like one before. That look in your eyes when I said that shit earlier bothered me all day and I had every intention of coming over to apologize to you, anyway. My mama would've had me cut a switch if she'd heard how I spoke to you. She's been telling me I need to 'adjust my attitude' for years now." He hesitated, as if unsure as to whether he wanted to finish his thought or not. "Ever since my uncle died back in the day."

I noticed how his jaw clenched automatically. "You were close to him?"

"Extremely. He was like a dad to me. Mine was in and out until he stopped pretending to be 'in' at all. But I never even felt like I was missing anything, thanks to Unc. He was everything. Made time for me. Taught me how to be a man. He's the main reason I joined the Army. But..." Jalil heaved a sigh as he briefly rubbed a hand across the back of his neck. "A routine stop at the gas station turned out to be the wrong place at the wrong time. He got jacked, stabbed, and left for dead like he was nothing. I was thirteen. And...I was in the car when it happened."

I gasped, tears immediately springing to my eyes. "Jalil..."

"Had nightmares for years. Became suspicious of everybody. Can't say I ever totally got over it." Jalil looked like he was fighting emotions at the memory. I could see him on the verge of crumbling but he caught himself, running a hand down his face a couple times as he cleared his throat. "Especially since they never caught the bastards who did it."

"Oh my god, Jalil...and you've been mad at the world ever since," I concluded, feeling like I understood him so much more now. I was full-on crying. "I can't even imagine how that must've been for you."

He looked at me, his expression softening with an appreciative smile. He cupped my face, wiping my tears with his thumb. "Kia, don't cry. 'Cause then you'll have me crying too and I'm trying to keep it together. There are still plenty of nights I break down when I let myself dwell on it too much. And I've lost enough smooth points with you already."

I laughed, pleasantly surprised that he was able to make jokes after recalling such a tragic experience. "I just hate you had to go through that. Losing a loved one is hard enough but to lose them like *that*..."

"You're tellin' me." He reluctantly slid his hand from my face and my eyes trailed it longingly, instantly missing his touch. "I didn't want to talk about it; really, I didn't want to talk, period. I just...shut down. And even after I started trying to get on with life, the anger and resentment stuck...it just became easier to lean into it than to have to explain what was behind it. I'm fully aware of my reputation but it's not anything I'm proud of."

"But you're still here. And you recognize that's not a healthy way to be and can do something about it. It's not too late. And you can further honor your uncle's memory by continuing to work on yourself and being the man he was raising you to be."

When his eyes sharpened, I worried that I'd overstepped, but he actually gave a conceding nod. "I've never thought of it like that, sadly."

"Jalil..." I gently nudged his shoulder with mine. "You were blessed with thirteen great years with him; I'm sure there are plenty of positive memories in there for you to lean on when you're having a moment. And it's okay to have those moments; you're human. You just can't let them consume you."

His lips slowly spread into a smile that almost made him look like a different person, it was so unfamiliar. "There's that pixie dust again. It's crazy that I actually feel...encouraged now. Hopeful, even. I'm trippin' that I even opened up to you about all that; some of my friends don't even know as much as I just told you. Plenty of people have tried to talk sense into me but you...the fact that you care enough to put *any* energy towards helping me after I showed my ass to you twice in two days says a lot about you. I might just have to pinch you to make sure you're real."

I giggled though when his hand landed on my forearm and gave it a light squeeze, a delicious tingly heat spread up my arm and over the rest of me like wildfire. Before he could retract his hand, I placed mine over his, chewing my bottom lip as we locked eyes. Our shoulders pressed together.

"Looks like we're *both* feeling better, then," I softly surmised, silently marveling at my open flirtatiousness. That wasn't usually like me but, hey, I'd already acted outside of myself once that day. "'Cause you're definitely doing something for me right now, too."

His grip on my arm tightened as his eyes briefly dropped to my lips. I suddenly wanted him to kiss me more than I wanted that oyster dressing earlier.

"I'm glad. 'Cause I'm seriously feeling better than I have in years." The drop in his voice only turned up the dial on my growing ache. "Thanks to you."

I wanted to jump him. I swear I did. And I hated that I didn't quite have *that* much nerve.

"There are so many more pleasurable ways to feel than sadness or anger." My voice had melted to practically a whisper. Now I was looking at *his* lips. "Wouldn't you say?"

"Hell yeah," he responded immediately, his jaws clenching again though I suspected this time for different reasons. "And I definitely prefer...pleasure."

The heat steadily built as we sat there, each silently challenging the other to make the first move. Our chests were heaving almost in unison and our grips on each other were tightening by the second. I'd never yearned for anything as much as I did for Jalil Dunn in that moment.

A silent countdown ticked in my head as I worked up the nerve to take his lips...then the moment broke.

"Um..." He cleared his throat, his eyes falling from mine as he eased back. "May I use your restroom?"

I blinked, snapping out of my momentary lustful trance. "Yeah, of course. It's right back there, on the left."

Slowly retracting his hand from under mine, he stood and rounded the couch, out of my vision. As soon as I heard the bathroom door close, I grabbed a pillow and smacked it against my forehead before burying my face in it, giving a muted scream as my knees bounced like beans on a hot skillet. My head told me that flirting with Jalil was foolish, especially when we were both clearly emotional, but the rest of me was fussing for letting that moment we shared pass without taking the kiss we both clearly wanted. Me and my stupid countdown.

But I missed my chance. And shaking it off wasn't as easy as I wanted it to be.

Now antsy, I shot off the couch and took my uneaten food to the kitchen before busying myself needlessly rearranging the picture frames on top of the short bookshelf near the door. My hands were actually shaking. I took a few deep breaths and assured myself that my fumble wasn't a big deal. If Jalil still wanted to hang out once he finished in the bathroom, I'd just suggest we watch a movie or something, offer him some wine, and just ride out the rest of this Christmas on an even higher note than we each started it. And maybe with our renewed understanding of each other, and with us being neighbors and all, we could even be friends from there on out.

Jalil rejoined me and despite what I'd just told myself, that ache for him reignited. I became more aware of his cologne and an image of burying my face in his neck as I rubbed my body against his flashed through my mind. I just hoped he wasn't about to tell me he had to go all of a sudden.

"Oh damn, is that what I think it is?"

I glanced at him and, noticing he was looking above my head, turned my eyes upward. I could almost feel the blood immediately rush to my face, already feeling silly.

"Oh…" I tore my eyes from the mistletoe we were standing under. I'd totally forgotten I'd put that up there. "Yeah…that was for the guy I was dating, but he didn't even notice it. And with everything that ended up happening, I just forgot to take it down."

Jalil looked at me with intrigue and concern. "What do you mean? What happened?"

"Ugh…he ghosted me last night. It was actually after you and I ran into each other that I realized it; I came back and he had left without a word. Still haven't heard from him. Actually, he blocked me. *And* he took my leftovers from our date. It didn't help that this was after we slept together for the first time."

My eyes immediately bugged and I ducked my head. Why the heck did I tell him that?? I hadn't even told Marlow about that yet. I *so* wanted to just dissipate into thin air right then. But Jalil gently grabbed my chin, lifting my face back up to meet his.

"Don't you dare hang your head. He's a fucking bum," Jalil declared with surprising intensity. Even his frown had returned, though now, I was flattered by it since it was on my behalf. "It's stuff like that that makes it hard to like people. Dating you until he got what he wanted and then disappearing like a bitch. And on Christmas Eve, at that."

I hadn't thought about it like that but maybe that was Gary's M.O. the whole time; get the panties, then move on to the next one. It wasn't a realization I loved but that wasn't my main concern at the moment.

"Yeah, it stung but a man like that doesn't deserve my tears," I declared with a slight shrug. I twisted a faux loc around my finger. "I wasn't in love with him or anything. He's clearly not the one for me, if he'd do something like that. If I feel foolish at all, it's that I actually hung *mistletoe*, trying to be romantic. You probably think that's incredibly cor-"

My words were cut off by Jalil's lips on mine. He hooked an arm around my waist, pulling me to him. It wasn't a forceful kiss but it was full of intention, our mouths opening slightly to each other and drawing out this introduction for several seconds.

He pulled back to look at me, silently asking if it was okay to proceed. My fingertips grazed his cheeks before I brought his face back to mine, making it crystal clear we were on the same page. His other arm wrapped around me as our tongues started playing with each other, no tentativeness or reservations to be found. And when he started moaning and gripping me through my sweats, I almost lost whatever composure I had left.

My hands gripped his sweater as he started walking me backwards towards the couch, our kiss never breaking. I pulled him on top of me, my leg lifting around his waist. Good lord, he felt amazing; his body was so solid and muscular. I already loved how his hands felt.

And I could pretty much say the same for that certain part pressing between my legs.

Neither of us was in any hurry. We made out like neither of us had any place to be, and if I had, I'd have gladly cancelled it. Part of me couldn't even believe Jalil Dunn was actually on top of me, savoring my lips like an entrée and doing a subtle grind that danced with mine. This was a far cry from my experience with Gary the night before, which had been light on the passion, to put it mildly. With Jalil, though...the way he whispered between kisses and squeezed by body and didn't try to rush to the next part assured me that tonight was going to have a much better ending.

"Can I touch you, Kia?" he asked against my lips.

"You can touch any and everything on me, Jalil. Repeatedly."

He actually growled and my entire body responded. The dampness in my panties was unmistakable and my nipples pebbled so hard they ached.

I gasped as his tongue slid down the side of my neck as his hand took hold of my breast. My thick sweater was pushed up as he eased his way down my body, kissing and licking and nipping my soft stomach as one hand gripped the side of my pants, pulling them down far enough to expose my hip. Who knew such an spot was an erogenous zone, because I shuddered *hard* when he started tongue-kissing that whole area.

"Jalil..." My body was writhing pretty much on its own by then, enjoying every second of what he was doing. I wanted him to explore all of me, twice. "Oh my gosh, that feels amazing..."

"You deserve to feel amazing."

His hands slid underneath my cotton sports bra that I usually wore when I was just sitting around the house. I was too aroused to be embarrassed that it was a little raggedy and had a couple of holes in it. He didn't seem to care about that, anyway. "You deserve everything, baby."

I screamed in pleasure when his lips finally got to my breasts. He suckled softly as if he just knew that's what I liked (it was), twirling his tongue around my nipples and moaning the whole time as if he was getting as much enjoyment from it as I was. My hands gripped his head, his sweater, the sides of the couch...I was coming undone. And the fact that he was being so methodical with it only added to the delicious torture.

He suddenly pulled back up to my face, laying a hungry kiss on me that I returned with equal energy.

"I want you, Kia," he informed, his voice gruff. His eyes were looking right into mine, the intensity only pumping up my arousal. "I want to take you to your bedroom. Take off all your clothes. Put my face between your legs so I can greedily devour you. Do it again. Then I want to get inside you and stay there for as long as you can take it. I want to spend the rest of this Christmas learning your body. And you damn sure don't have to worry about me dipping out afterwards." He slow-licked his bottom lip, hunger darkening his eyes. "What do you think about that?"

When I tell you I'd never been more turned on in my *life*, on every level, I *mean* that.

"I think we'd better get to the bedroom," I told him, almost not recognizing my own voice. "Because I damn sure want all of that and whatever you haven't told me about yet."

FOUR

THAT DANG MISTLETOE.

I never would have guessed when I hung it to entice Gary that it would instead lead to me being sweaty and naked underneath Jalil Dunn. And let me tell you, that man keeps his word. Everything he said he wanted to do, he not only did but excelled at it.

Usually my first time with a man involved lots of nerves and second-guessing on my part. I wasn't typically self-conscious, but I always wondered what they would *really* think about my size twelve body that was adorned with more than a few stretch marks and had a little jiggle to it. Especially with Jalil, since I was less than half that size when he knew me back in the day. I actually loved my grown woman body, especially since I always hated how skinny I used to be. And while I knew it was the empowered thing to say that I didn't care what the man thought as long as I was satisfied with myself, truth be told, I cared a teeny tiny bit.

But Jalil's eyes only got hungrier as my clothes came off. He had to touch or kiss or lick just about every new part he exposed, making it clear he was more than satisfied with what he saw.

"Gotdamn Kia, you are driving me crazy already," he breathed, shooting up to give me an impassioned kiss, taking my face in his hands. He'd been sliding my pants down and left them pooled around my ankles in his urge to slob me down. "I want all of you, baby, all night. 'Cause I already know I won't be able to get enough of you."

"I don't want you to get enough." My hands pulled at his sweater, hating that it was keeping me from touching him. "I'm all yours tonight, Jalil."

"That's what I wanted to hear. Let's get you off that ankle."

He lifted me and placed me onto the bed, even though I could've just laid down on my own. I certainly wasn't complaining. Nor was I even thinking about my sore ankle or the fact that I wasn't wearing any of my cute panties. My raw arousal had boxed out any lingering self-consciousness or nerves I might've had.

Once he finished removing my clothes, Jalil got naked for me. And he did me the pleasure of doing it slowly while I laid there braced on my elbows, blatantly enjoying the show.

"Gosh, you look delicious, Jalil," I purred, my legs rubbing together in anticipation. His body was the stuff of fantasies. A light film of chest hair between some amazing pecs, bulging biceps each covered in tattoos, quads that almost seemed unreal. I was going to be dreaming about this man. "I'm definitely enjoying this show but I need you to hurry up..."

"So you still want this, then?" He tossed his pants aside and started stroking himself. My kitty tingled, just ready to handle all of that. "If you've changed your mind or have any doubts at all, please tell me now, Kia."

"I haven't changed my mind and I'm not doubting anything. Now get on top of me."

And that he did.

Jalil indeed spent the rest of the night learning my body. He took his time savoring every inch. His tongue and fingers were on a mission to find any and every spot that made me moan or shudder or wanna shoot off the bed. And I had a lot more than I thought.

"Jalil!" I breathed, clutching his head as he dove in for his second helping of my kitty. I was still super sensitive from the first one but he concentrated on the surrounding parts, letting me calm down. As if. "Jalil, yes..."

"*So* good," he whispered, looking up at me as the tip of his tongue traced along my thigh junction. "Fuck, this is so good."

And it got even better once he was finally inside of me. Now we were *both* shuddering.

"Kia..." His voice was shaky, his breath hot against my neck. "You good, baby?"

"Oh yes. *Hell* yes." I bit my bottom lip to hold in my scream. "I'm more than good."

I wasn't lying. The way Jalil sexed me had me forgetting about all my troubles. And just like everything leading up to it, he took his time. He wasn't just boning so he could get his. He seemed to really want me to have the best experience I could possibly have, and he was delivering. It was intense, impassioned, and intentional. The heat steadily increased as time ticked on and the sky darkened outside my dull window, and after a while we were both sauna sweaty, having changed positions several times by then. It was *so* amazingly sexy.

"I'm about to come, baby... Jalil..."

He just guided my arms around his neck and began stroking harder, making my voice get lost in my throat. My mouth hung open as I held onto him as if for dear life, loving that his ferocity was increasing the closer I got.

"Come for me, Kia," he ordered. "I'm already addicted to making you come; the look in your eyes, the way you shiver under my hands, how you scream my name...you're so fucking sexy. I need to see it again, baby."

He was going to get his wish. Several strokes later, that blazing explosion took over my body and I screamed his name over and over until my screams melted into whimpers. He grabbed my chin and held it as he blessed me with a deep kiss, the yummy sloppy noisy lip-smacking kind.

Jalil stayed on top of me as we both tried to catch our breaths. A goofy smile threatened to shoot across my face. I was floating. My body hadn't had this kind of activity in a while and I was sure I'd be sore the next day but I'd gladly deal with it. Forget going to the gym; there wasn't a workout invented that felt as good as this.

"I don't wanna get off you," Jalil admitted, nuzzling my cheek. "But I will if you need me to."

My fingers clutched his sweaty back, keeping him close. "You don't hear me complaining."

"You're really amazing, you know that?" He pulled back to look at me, affection softening his eyes. "And I'm not just talking about the bomb-ass sex we just had. I mean *you*."

A different kind of heat flushed over me. "You don't have to say that, Jalil."

"You think I'm bullshitting you?"

"Well, it's been an emotional evening for both of us. And you *are* still inside of me..."

"Kia, if this was just about sex, I'd be heading out the door already. I've sincerely enjoyed this evening with you; it's the first time in forever that I wasn't thinking about any of the shit that plagues my mind day in and day out. I felt comfortable enough with you to open up like I haven't done with anyone else. I actually feel optimistic, and I haven't felt that since I was a kid. More than that, I'm just..." His finger traced my collarbone before he looked into my eyes. "I'm feeling something real here, baby. And I'm not gonna dismiss that."

Just when my heart rate started to calm down.

Part of me wanted to tell Jalil to wait until he was completely off his sex high to tell me that. And that I should wait until I was off mine to respond. But the other part, the one I listened to, wasn't going to let another moment pass me by.

"I'm not either, Jalil," I admitted, a cool blast going off inside of me at the admission. I caressed his face, feeling everything shift inside me. "You and me...this feels more right than anything has in a while. And I don't want it to stop."

He grinned, and I instantly knew I wanted to keep making him do that. His smile was too beautiful for him not to show it more.

"I'm gonna say something really corny now," he playfully warned, his brow arched slightly. "Prepare yourself."

I wiggled underneath him, giggling when he grunted in response. "All set."

"I mainly moved into this building because it was closer to work and the VA, but I wasn't totally happy about it because I preferred where I was. But between rent hikes and traffic getting worse thanks to so many people moving here to Brodence, I felt I didn't have much choice. But now...I feel like I was put here for a reason. Like God had my gift waiting right down the hall from me."

"Aww Jalil!" My goofy smile was on full blast as I brought his face to mine for a kiss. Corny or not, I loved that and wanted to hear more of it. I wanted to date this man. I wanted more nights in bed with him. I wanted what I thought I wanted with Gary.

I was starting to feel pretty optimistic, myself. And it was genuine, not just something I was making myself believe.

"Is that okay for me to say?" he asked softly, still nipping at my lips. "I want to always be honest with you, Kia. I want you to trust me. And I'll earn that. Just know that whatever I tell you will be sincere. As I've already shown, I can be a little *too* straightforward."

We both laughed at the reminder of that morning, which by then felt like eons ago.

"It's totally okay to say." I smiled against his lips, still wondering if I was going to wake up at any second. "I'm here for all the corny declarations."

"Remember you said that."

When Christmas rolled into the day after, I was still cuddled up with Jalil. We'd sat up talking (and occasionally fooling around), including me sharing everything I'd been through the past year and a half, until our extremely long days finally caught up to us and we dozed off. When morning light hit and I woke up trying to remember what time I had to be at work, then remembered that I was probably out of a job, there was no panic. I untangled myself from Jalil and went to find my phone, and as expected, Vinny had sent me a text letting me know that while he understood why I flipped out like I did, he couldn't let me come back there. I was surprisingly okay with it.

"Kia."

"I'm out here."

Jalil shuffled into the living room, wiping the sleep from his eyes. "Everything okay?"

I heaved a resigned sigh and tossed my phone onto the couch. "Yeah. My waitressing days are over, though. At least at that diner."

"Damn. I was hoping they'd give you a break."

"I expected to get canned. And it was far from a dream job. I'm sure I'll find something else."

"You will." His voice held so much certainty that it actually jarred me a little. "I'm keeping hope alive."

"I'll take all the good vibes I can get."

Jalil had some things to do that day so he had to go, but invited me over to his place later that afternoon, which I readily accepted. Once we both got freshened up a little, he walked me under the mistletoe again and pulled me in for a kiss that lasted for a good couple minutes.

"You gonna take that down?" he muttered, glancing up towards the mistletoe.

"I was but now...I think I'm going to leave it up there. It's what kicked all this off, after all. And it's another excuse for us to make out."

He laughed. "Yeah, this is gonna be good."

I grinned, knowing I was ready to explore whatever was going to come up with Jalil.

By New Years, we were officially a couple. A few days after that, he referred me for an executive assistant position at his friend's brokerage firm, and I got the job.

Hardly a night went by when he wasn't in my apartment or I wasn't in his.

On Valentine's Day, he told me he loved me for the first time. And I was right there with him on that because I surely loved him, too.

By Independence Day, we were practically living together. I knew I wanted Jalil all day every day but I was more than happy to just take things as they came. We were both thriving with renewed outlooks on life, and I was insanely grateful for that.

But Jalil had made it abundantly clear that he had more intentions for us than just dating. Even asked if I'd like a Christmas wedding (I would). He dropped plenty of hints that a ring would be coming any day.

And on August thirty-first, my birthday, surrounded by my family at my parents' house, I got it.

Mrs. Kia Dunn, coming right up.

And that mistletoe was indeed *still* up in my apartment.

AAAAND THAT'S IT! I hope you enjoyed *From Meltdown to Mistletoe*. I wanted to do a holiday short and I thought about bringing back one of my previous couples, but decided to introduce somebody new. Don't be surprised if you see Kia and Jalil again at some point.

However you felt about this story, please leave a review on Amazon and/or Goodreads. Reviews are soooo vital for us indie authors. ☺

If you haven't already, feel free to subscribe to my sporadic newsletter at www.jessicaterry.com[1]. You can also find me on Twitter/X at @ItsJessicaTerry, and on Instagram, TikTok, and Facebook at @AuthorJessicaTerry. Hang with me. ☺

---

1.   http://www.jessicaterry.com/

Also by Jessica Terry

Some Like 'em Thick

It's All Right...Now

Not By a Long Shot

Get Right

Decisions and Consequences

Take One For the Team

When You Share Too Much

Backtalk

Emasculated

Restless

The Beginning of Again

Always and Nevers

She is Me

Split By the Bell

The Karma Call

Forehead Kiss

All Because of Ava

Love Intolerant

Mr. Time Waster

The Stubborn Kind

The Introvert Series

An Introvert's Christmas
Wooing the Introvert
The Introvert Roast
I, Take Thee Introvert
The Introvert Series Compilation (paperback only)

J ust for fun, here's the first chapter of my dislike-to-lovers romance, *Always and Nevers*. ☺

ONE

Jerome already knew his first date with Courtney might be his last. If he wanted to hear a woman spend the evening bitching about another man, he'd hang out with his mother.

They were only halfway through dinner and most of Courtney's conversation centered around something to do with her ex-boyfriend, Clint. How the restaurant reminded her of their first date. How Clint wore the same kind of cologne Jerome wore. How Clint had flat feet.

Jerome wasn't even sure how that one had come up.

What he *did* know, though, was that he was over this whole date.

"I'm about ready to call it a night," he announced before she could launch into another story about her ex. He eyed her half-eaten salmon then looked at her pointedly. "You done?"

"Oh...already?" Courtney looked disappointed. "I thought we were having such a nice time."

"I have to get up real early tomorrow."

Her honey-toned eyes drifted to some spot over Jerome's shoulder. "That's wild that you said that."

"Why?"

"That started to be Clint's excuse when he was trying to get away. Turned out he was just going to meet his little side chick."

"Hmm." Jerome motioned to the waiter for the check and looked at his watch.

"But I'm sure *you* wouldn't do anything like that," she quickly added, turning her attention back to him. "All men aren't the same, right?"

"Right. Yeah."

"It took me a while before I could say I really got past what Clint did," Courtney mused as she mindlessly raked her fork through her food. "But I knew I'd have to get over it or else I'd never find a good relationship."

I hope you don't think you've found one over here, Jerome thought wryly.

"Thank God I've gotten myself together. You have no idea how much of a mess I was after I broke up with him."

"Yeah, you've got your shit together, all right," Jerome muttered as he slapped some cash into the leather envelope the waiter had just brought over and handed it back to him before he could walk off.

"Oh my god, you have *no* idea how much I needed to hear that!" Courtney gushed as Jerome stood. She followed suit, grinning as she rounded the table and followed him towards the exit. "Sometimes I wonder if he's really out of my system or not but it's good to know I'm totally over it."

Jerome didn't bother responding. He just opened his passenger side door for her and admonished himself for getting sucked in by a belly ring and a nice rack.

He could've just been honest and told Courtney that she was talking about her ex-boyfriend too much, but had already decided he didn't care enough to bother. After tonight, he didn't plan on seeing her again. It just served as another reminder that most women had more issues than *Essence* magazine.

Courtney was thankfully quiet on the way back to her apartment. She just sat in the passenger seat mindlessly twirling her maple brown hair around her finger and looking out the window. Jerome had to stop himself from stealing too many glances at her thick thighs, complete with a humongous flower tattoo, underneath her short red dress. Annoying or not, she had the kind of body he loved: curvy with a tilt towards voluptuous. He should've just slept with her and gone on about his business instead of trying something different and courting her.

When they got to her place, Courtney placed a hand on his arm, smiling.

"I appreciate it, Jerome."

"You're welcome."

"I know you said you have to get up early tomorrow, but...you wanna come in for a little while? I won't keep you too long."

Jerome started to say no, but he recognized that gleam in her eye. She wasn't inviting him in just to talk.

"Yeah, okay," he acquiesced, killing the engine. "For a little bit."

Thankfully, Courtney didn't try to prolong things by subjecting Jerome to small talk or time-wasting offers of something to drink. She figured there was only one sure way to get him to forget about the time for a while, so as soon as they were through her front door, she grabbed his hand and led him to her bedroom.

They shared their first kiss, Courtney wrapping her arms around his neck and roaming her hands across his smooth bald head. Jerome readily returned her kiss, his hands sliding down to grab handfuls of her round backside. She squirmed when his lips slid to her neck, and he figured he'd discovered one of her spots. The more he concentrated his attention there, the louder her groans and grunts became. Pretty soon, she was pushing him down onto her frilly flowered comforter.

"Still have to get up early?" she asked him with an arched brow, hiking up her dress.

"Yeah, I do. So we'd better not waste any time."

Getting the message, Courtney seductively but swiftly shimmied out of her tight dress, then her strapless lace bra and panties. When she was in nothing but her black peep-toe booties, she crawled onto the bed and on top of Jerome. In the next couple of minutes, his clothes were on the floor next to hers and he was tearing open a condom wrapper with his teeth.

"Oh god," Courtney panted as they were in the throes, her nails digging into his back. "You feel so *amazing*!"

Jerome just grunted, never having been one to say much during sex. But he was glad she was enjoying it and rewarded her praise with a deep kiss and a deeper stroke. Courtney squealed so loudly that Jerome thought he might have hurt her in some way.

"Please don't stop!" she pleaded, clamping her limbs around him. She made an array of strange noises as Jerome continued to pump into her, either not minding or noticing that except for some pants and groans, he was practically mute.

Flipping him onto his back, Courtney began to ride Jerome, facing him and then swiveling around and treating him to some reverse cowgirl action. Jerome hissed at the sight of her ample bottom bouncing up and down on him, and grabbed her hips with his rough fingers. He was just glad she was being quiet.

But of course, that only lasted so long.

"Oooh," she moaned, grinding her hips in way that Jerome knew would be replayed in future fantasies. "Oh god, Clint, you are *so* good..."

Jerome stopped moving. Did she just call him Clint?

Oh, hell no, he thought.

Courtney didn't seem to notice her slip-up, and Jerome considered that the final nail in the coffin of whatever this was they were doing. He'd just get his, get out, and chalk this one up as another failure.

When they finished, Jerome laid there with Courtney strewn across him, half-asleep. He checked his watch, then gently eased her arm from his chest and slid off the bed, picking up his clothes.

She stirred, easing her eyes open briefly. "You leaving?"

"Yeah."

"You want some water or something before you go?"

"I'm good, thanks."

"Call me tomorrow, okay?"

Jerome didn't want to commit to something he knew he wouldn't do, so he just finished getting dressed and leaned down to kiss her forehead. "Get some sleep."

"M'kay." Courtney turned to her side and curled into a ball. She sighed contently and smiled, her eyes still closed. "Talk to you soon, Clint."

Jerome just glared at her and shook his head.

Well, he thought. *At least the sex was good.*

JEROME TRIED TO PUT Courtney and their wack date out of his mind as he went about work the next day. The clothing store he managed, Iced Denim, was rather full, which was nothing new for a Saturday afternoon. As much as he usually enjoyed his job, he would have liked to be home watching the string of football games that were on instead of just getting score updates on his phone or quick stop-ins to look at the small television in the back office.

His store was really popular with the young crowd and while they often brought a lot of business, they often brought a lot of headache, too. Jerome had to constantly keep an eye on them to make sure that nothing walked out of the store, even with the visible security cameras and ink security tags that most of the merchandise was affixed with. Some people just didn't care and tried to make a run for it anyway, rarely getting very far. Then Jerome had to deal with the aftermath and the paperwork, sometimes the police, and he just hoped he'd get a break from all of that today.

If only people would just do what they know they're supposed to do. And *not* do what they know they're *not* supposed to do.

The day was about halfway over when Jerome's brother Dodge came by. Dodge was the product of an affair Jerome's father Gibson had when Jerome was a baby, and despite the turmoil and drama that it caused between Gibson and his wife Goldie, Jerome and Dodge had always been close.

"What's up, brother?" Dodge greeted Jerome along with a brief hug.

"Hey, man. What you doing over here?"

"Wanted to come get that hat I had my eye on the other day. The blue one with the silver trim?"

"Oh yeah, I put one behind the counter for you. Draya will get it for you when you go up there. Those things have been selling out ever since we got them."

"Good looking out on that. Do I get a hookup on the price, too?"

"No."

"Damn." Dodge looked around the store. "Y'all are busy up in here today. Oh yeah, how did that date of yours go last night? What was her name, Mya?"

"*Courtney.*"

"Whatever. How was it?"

"It was a waste of time, that's what it was. She was nice and everything, but she's not over her ex. Kept bringing him up and comparing everything to something they did together."

"Oh hell no. I hate that. I would've left her sitting there and had her call her ex to come get her."

"I actually believe you would do that, too. But I just figured I wouldn't call her anymore after that. Especially after she called me by his name while I was at her spot."

"I was hoping you'd say you at least got the draws. So the night wasn't a *total* waste. But she called you the wrong name, too?"

"Yep. Twice."

"Oooh-wee. I can't front like I've never done that, though. There's been a few times when I said *Brianna* instead of *Beretta* or something like that and had to try to play it off."

"Who the hell is named Beretta?"

"It's just an example, man. The point is I know how that can go. The ladies don't care for that at all so I *know* it pissed you off."

"It annoyed me but it's not like I'm in a relationship with her; if she was my woman, I would've been majorly pissed off. After we finished I just got my shit and left."

"Has she tried to call you today?"

"Yeah. And she sent a bunch of texts. I haven't responded to any of it."

"Man, if you want *my* opinion—"

"When do I ever ask for your opinion?"

"—I'd say just keep her around for when you want to get broke off," Dodge continued, ignoring Jerome's statement. "You know, put her in the booty call rotation."

"I don't have a *booty call rotation*, Dodge. That's your shit, not mine."

"I bet you wish you had one some nights. You haven't had a woman since Holyfield was champ."

"That's real funny. But keeping Courtney around just on the casual tip might not be a bad idea. As long as we both stay on the same page as far as what the real deal is, it could work."

"It could, as long as she doesn't start catching feelings, like a lot of 'em do. They *say* they can handle just being a cut buddy but it's only a matter of time before they start talking about how they're 'feeling differently' and 'want to see where it can go.' That's why I don't do relationships at all."

"You have a girlfriend, Dodge."

"And as far as she knows, I'm totally faithful to her. No need in ruining that."

Jerome shook his head. Dodge was just like everyone else in his family; they seemed to be allergic to monogamy. They might get into a relationship with someone, but forget about them being faithful. Jerome's parents had been cheating on each other ever since he could remember. Every cousin he had was a player. And Dodge couldn't seem to resist indulging in whatever pretty thing batted their eyelashes at him.

"I don't get how a brotha as educated as yourself has such a warped mindset when it comes to women," Jerome stated, waving to a couple who entered the store. He noted how they were hand-in-hand and looked completely comfortable with each other. He couldn't help but wonder how long they'd been together, and if either of them had stepped out on the other. "When did everyone get so jaded?"

Dodge scoffed. "I'm not jaded. I just think monogamy is bullshit."

"How is it bullshit for two people to commit to each other?"

"Okay, maybe it's not *bullshit*, but it's unrealistic. I just don't believe it's healthy to put so much faith and trust in one person like that. People are always gonna disappoint you. So why even go there?"

"So why are you with Yolonda, then? 'Cause I bet she doesn't share this philosophy of yours."

"Yolonda is good people. I care about her. I'm just not tryin' to marry her or anything."

"And I hope to high heaven she doesn't wanna marry *you*."

"Hell, I hope she doesn't, too. Marriage is a whole 'nother subject. Nobody *really* wants to be bound to somebody else for life. Look at Dad and Goldie. How many times have they cheated on each other just this *week*??"

"I think Dad has Mama by one right now."

"See there? Why even bother with all that?"

"I guess they have their reasons. I just know it *would* be nice to have a steady woman but it's hard to trust folks nowadays. Everybody seems to have some baggage or drama or issues."

"Hmph, well if you're waiting on somebody who doesn't have any of that, then you might as well get ready to die alone." Dodge checked his phone. "I'm gonna head out in a second; I have to go meet somebody later. And don't forget that Yolonda wants us to meet up for dinner with her after you close."

"I didn't forget."

"Good. Now I won't have to hear her whine about it."

"Uh-huh. Meeting another one of your students looking for extra credit?"

Dodge grinned, not being able to help it. "I don't know what you're talking about. And anyway, the good thing about being a college professor is that all of my students are grown."

"You're still not supposed to be fraternizing with them, though, and you know that. Sometimes I think you *wanna* get fired."

"It's all about the thrill, brother," Dodge claimed, giving Jerome some dap.

Jerome shook his head but couldn't resist smiling. His brother would never change.

"Hey, stop!"

Jerome and Dodge whipped their heads around to see two kids racing towards the exit. The brothers instinctively separated and each managed to catch one of the kids before they darted out the door.

"Hey, let us go!"

Draya, Jerome's employee who had yelled at them, rushed over.

"I saw her take the backs off the earrings and put them in her pockets," she informed, pointing to the girl in Jerome's grasp. She turned her eyes to the boy that was trying to get away from Dodge. "And this one rolled up some socks and stuffed them down his crotch."

If this was a television show, Jerome would have thought that was funny. It was anything but, now. The kids couldn't have been more than nine or ten years old. And when he peered closer at the boy Dodge was holding, he realized he knew him.

"Brandon?"

The boy looked away. Dodge looked back and forth between them, surprised.

"You know who this is?"

"Yeah, man. It's our cousin."

"It is?" Dodge asked incredulously, taking another look at the boy.

"Yeah. He's like our third cousin on Dad's side. His mama is Donita, the one that's always posting her cupcakes on Instagram."

"What? She shows that kind of stuff and you still follow her?"

Jerome cut his eyes at him. "*Actual* cupcakes, professor."

"Oh."

"Brandon, who brought you over here? And who is this girl you got with you?"

Brandon stayed defiantly silent.

"Boy, don't think I won't jack you up. If you're bold enough to come in here trying to steal, you can answer for it when you get caught. Now start talking 'cause I'm not gonna ask you again."

Knowing Jerome meant business, Brandon sucked his teeth and replied, "Donita dropped us off. And this is my girlfriend, Kira."

Jerome didn't know which to address first; the fact that his little cousin called himself having a girlfriend or that he called his mother by her first name.

Shaking his head, he jerked his head towards the back of the store, and said to Dodge, "Let's get them back to the office. Thanks, Draya."

After the two would-be thieves were seated in his office, Dodge went back to the sales floor while Jerome tracked down Donita's number. He was going to just have her come get the kids, get his merchandise back, and call it a draw.

What he *didn't* expect, though, was Donita to turn the tables on him.

"Are you seriously keeping my boy over some damn socks?" she barked at him. "We're supposed to be family!"

Jerome gaped. He didn't know Donita all *that* well but he didn't expect this reaction. "Family or not, they don't need to be in here stealing."

"You should just give them that stuff. It's not like they tried to steal some shoes or something major. You wouldn't even miss that tiny stuff they took."

"Did you tell them to take this stuff?"

"No!"

"So you don't see *anything* wrong with them taking what doesn't belong to them, huh? Is that what I'm hearing?"

"I didn't say all that. I just said you shouldn't be making it such a big deal."

"You're sitting up here fussing at me 'cause I stopped them from stealing, so don't say that's not what you meant. And anyway, I didn't throw them in the back of a damn cop car. I called their parents, like we usually do with minors who steal."

"And *I'm* saying you could've just let them go. Maybe they needed that stuff. Did you consider that?"

His patience gone, Jerome stood from his desk. "Maybe if you were more worried about your boy instead of what color frosting you're gonna come up with next and what filter you're gonna use on Instagram, he might not feel the need to do this kind of stuff. But don't try to make me the bad guy for doing my job just because you clearly haven't been doing yours."

Donita gasped. "How dare you, Jerome!"

"How dare I, nothing. Now I suggest you come on and get this boy from my store. And know that I'm not gonna be as lenient if it happens again. Post *that*."

He hung up and made a call to the girl's parents, who were thankfully more mature about the situation and thanked him for letting them know what happened. They immediately came to retrieve their daughter, made her apologize to Jerome and return the stolen earrings, and insisted it wouldn't happen again. Donita eventually showed up to get Brandon, but she clearly had an attitude and stomped out of the store with nothing but a suck of her teeth and a roll of her eyes.

"Whatever," Jerome muttered, heading back out to the sales floor.

He was surprised to see Dodge still there, but he quickly saw the reason. Dodge was putting the moves on a cute woman with long braids and ridiculously thick false eyelashes. They each pulled out their phones, no doubt getting each other's numbers. Not surprised at all, Jerome just went on about his business.

A little after closing time, Jerome got a call from his father, Gibson. He almost didn't want to answer, since he had a feeling he knew what the call was for.

"I need you to cover for me tonight," Gibson requested, his voice rushed.

Jerome sighed. "I really wish y'all would stop calling me for this."

"You might not even need to say anything. But just in case Goldie *does* call you asking where I am, just tell her I had to go see about my aunt. Goldie hates her so I know she won't go over there after me."

"Aren't y'all a little old for his? It's not like y'all stepping out on each other is some kind of secret. Why are all the lies and stuff necessary?"

"I don't have time to go into all that right now, Jerome. Just tell her that if she calls."

"Whatever, Dad."

Hanging up the phone, Jerome tried hard to think of *one* person he was close to that wasn't a cheater. Besides maybe his grandfather, he couldn't.

Did you love *From Meltdown to Mistletoe*? Then you should read *Mrs. Soul Crusher*[1] by Jessica Terry!

'The main reason I'd agreed to marry Aurora - sex - was the very thing that was making me hate her.'

Montrel Burns knew he'd made a mistake marrying Aurora. But he figured he'd made his bed and he was stuck in it. Especially since choosing Aurora cost him the love of his life, Claire.

Aurora Chadwick loved Montrel...in her own way. Their marriage might not have been conventional but she wanted it to be. Yet every time she vowed to commit to being a 'real' wife to

---

1. https://books2read.com/u/bajVk2

2. https://books2read.com/u/bajVk2

Montrel, her urges overcame her and she ended up right back where she started.

Montrel had no idea he'd married a sex addict. And if that wasn't enough, he felt he was just wasting his life. Would he be able to get out and find direction before Aurora crushed his soul completely?

Content warning: Sex addiction, adultery, depression, brief mentions of STDs and suicide contemplation, and miscarriage.

Read more at https://www.jessicaterry.com/.

About the Author

Jessica Terry caught the writing bug at a young age and loves little more than holing up at home in Douglasville, GA, cranking out contemporary novels. And eating. www.jessicaterry.com

Read more at https://www.jessicaterry.com/.